EMMA BEAN

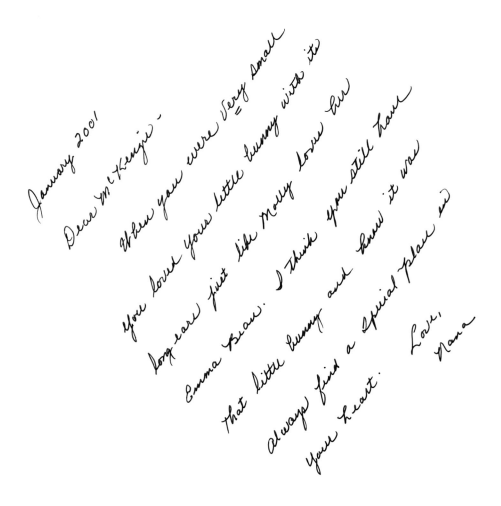

January 2001

Dear McKenzie -

When you were very small
you loved your little bunny with its
long ears just like Molly loves her
Emma Bean. I think you still have
that little bunny and know it was
always find a special place in
your heart. Love,
Nana

EMMA BEAN

Jean Van Leeuwen
Pictures by Juan Wijngaard

Dial Books for Young Readers  *New York*

For Bear and Sallie Rabbit and all the rest   J. V. L.
To Patricia, with love   J. W.

Published by Dial Books for Young Readers
A Division of Penguin Books USA Inc.
375 Hudson Street
New York, New York 10014

Text copyright © 1993 by Jean Van Leeuwen
Illustrations copyright © 1993 by Juan Wijngaard
All rights reserved
Printed in Hong Kong
by South China Printing Company (1988) Limited
Design by Nancy R. Leo
First Edition
3 5 7 9 10 8 6 4

Library of Congress Cataloging in Publication Data
Van Leeuwen, Jean.
Emma Bean / by Jean Van Leeuwen ; pictures by Juan Wijngaard.—1st ed.
p.   cm.
Summary: Emma Bean, a homemade toy rabbit, joins Molly at birth
and shares her trials and triumphs as she grows from infant to little girl.
ISBN 0-8037-1392-4.—ISBN 0-8037-1393-2 (lib. bdg.)
[1. Toys—Fiction.   2. Rabbits—Fiction.   3. Growth—Fiction.]
I. Wijngaard, Juan, ill.   II. Title.
PZ7.V3273Em 1993   [E]—dc20   92-29035   CIP   AC

The art for this book was prepared by using watercolors.
It was then color-separated and reproduced in red, yellow, blue, and black halftones.

Once there was a rabbit and she had a girl.
The girl's name was Molly.
The rabbit was Emma Bean.

Emma Bean was born on a summer night when the air was whispery soft and the moon shone silver through the treetops.

It shone into a room where someone was sewing.

Snip, snip. Scissors cut up scraps of long-ago dresses.

Stitch, stitch. A needle shaped a body, head, arms, and legs.

Then came the stuffing, made of rags. Black buttons for eyes. Whiskers that curled up like a smile. And the longest, floppiest ears a rabbit ever had.

"There," said a quiet voice.

Hands held Emma Bean close, there in the dark with the moon making lacy patterns on the floor.

Creak, creak. They rocked and waited, rocked and waited.

For days Emma Bean sat waiting in that rocking chair.

Then one morning the hands laid her gently inside a box. The lid came down, and everything was dark. A few minutes later the box began to travel.

Emma Bean bounced.

Emma Bean tumbled.

Emma Bean stood on her ears.

At last the box stopped moving. The lid was lifted up.

And there she was, face-to-face with a baby. It was no bigger than she was, and had fat cheeks and bright red hair that stuck straight up. Its mouth was wide open and it was crying. The noise was just terrible.

That was how Emma Bean met Molly.

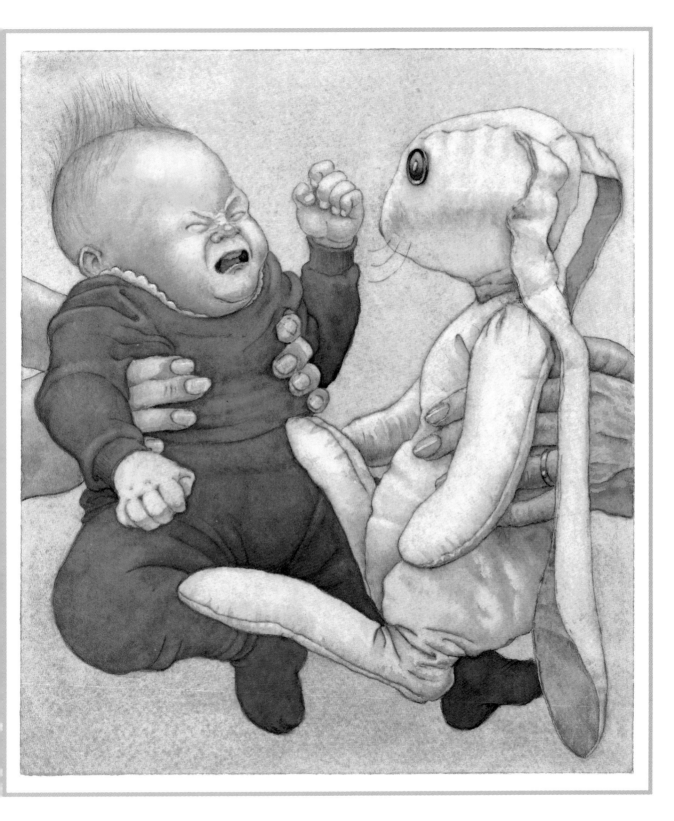

It could be said that Emma Bean's early life was hard.

She was sat on and spit up on and tossed out of Molly's crib onto the cold floor. At meal times her job was to taste things. Molly didn't like anything orange. Soon Emma Bean's pink nose became an orange nose.

But the worst times were when they went to the doctor's office.

"First we give your rabbit a shot," said the doctor. "Then Molly."

So Emma Bean was poked full of holes.

On her first birthday Molly had five teeth and a cloud of curly red hair and she could say "Da-da" and "Bye-bye." After lunch she walked from the chair to the coffee table for the first time.

After that wherever Molly went, Emma Bean went too. Molly carried her by the ears.

Yes, it was hard having Molly for her girl.

One day Molly was sitting in her high chair, chewing on a string bean and practicing her talking.

"Mmmm," she said, waving her bean. "Emmm. Emmm-ma."

"She said Mama!" cried Molly's mother.

Molly smiled proudly at her mother. Then she gave Emma Bean a taste of her string bean.

"Emmm-ma," she said. "Bean."

And that is what she called her forever after.

After dinner Molly and her father liked to play Toss the Bunny.

Molly tossed Emma Bean high in the air. Her father caught her. He tossed Emma Bean up and Molly caught her. Then they got fancy.

Emma Bean did cartwheels.

She touched the ceiling with her ears.

She did a triple somersault and Molly's father caught her by the toes.

Soaring through the air, ears flapping like a bird, Emma Bean looked down on the lamp, the hair on Molly's father's head, Molly's smiling face.

It was a wonderful thing to be flying.

Emma Bean had the most remarkable ears—long and soft and pink and floppy.

They were ears to tell secrets to. *Pssst—didyouknow—yesshedid.*

They were ears to sing songs to. *Twinkle twinkle up in a tree.*

And when the moon made spooky shadows on Molly's new big-girl bed, they were ears to whisper into, *"What's that?"*

Then Molly and Emma Bean burrowed under the blankets where nothing could find them. There they stayed, all cozy and warm, until Molly fell asleep, one of Emma Bean's ears flopped over her cheek.

Molly was three when she first discovered strawberries. Oh, they were fat and sweet and full of juice, just like the summer day.

"Mmm, yummy!" she said.

She gave Emma Bean a taste. "One for you," she said, "and one for me." Pretty soon they had eaten a whole bowlful.

"More, please," said Molly.

They ate so many that their hands and dresses and even their ears turned bright pink. And on their faces were great big strawberry smiles.

"Bath time!" said Molly's father. He handed her the soap.

"One for you," said Molly, "and one for me."

She scrubbed. She rubbed. Little by little the bathwater got pink.

And that was the end of their strawberry smiles.

One day Molly's mother took her to the zoo. Of course, Emma Bean went too. Of all the animals, Molly's favorites were the rabbits.

"They have ears like Emma Bean," she said. "And twitchy noses."

Molly twitched her nose. The rabbits twitched their noses.

Molly hopped. The rabbits hopped.

"Look, Mommy," she said. "I'm a rabbit."

But Molly's mother wasn't there.

"Mommy, where are you?" cried Molly.

Tears fell on Emma Bean's head. She was squeezed so tight, her stuffing almost popped. The two of them were all alone, without a mother.

Then suddenly Molly's mother was there again.

"We thought we lost you!" said Molly.

"Me too," said her mother. They held each other tight.

"Look," said Molly, twitching her nose. "I'm a rabbit."

"I can do that," said her mother.

So they all twitched noses and hopped with the rabbits at the zoo.

In the beginning Emma Bean had no clothes. Then Molly dressed her in the dress she wore when she was a baby.

Molly's mother found her some pajamas. Molly's grandmother knitted her a hat with ear holes. And one winter day Molly made her a snowsuit out of a woolly sock, a scrap of her baby blanket, and a safety pin.

By the time Emma Bean was four, she had overalls, a party dress, three necklaces, and hair ribbons for her ears.

Every morning when Molly woke up, she said, "What shall we wear today?"

Leaves were floating down from the sky the day Peter came to play.

Molly showed Peter how to play Toss the Bunny. Up flew Emma Bean. Up, up, she soared, higher than ever before. Only this time she didn't come down. She was caught in the outstretched fingers of a tree branch.

No one came to get her down.

After awhile clouds covered the sun. Raindrops fell—*plop, plop*—on Emma Bean's head. Night came, and a cold wind blew. Suddenly it caught Emma Bean by the ears. Up she sailed, somersaulting through the dark sky. Then down to earth she crashed.

Molly and her father found her there. In a moment Emma Bean was cradled in Molly's arms. And Molly was whispering, "I'm sorry."

Emma Bean had a broken arm, a torn ear, and several missing whiskers. She spent all the next day in bed. But after twelve stitches and seventeen hugs, she seemed a lot better.

Wherever Molly went, Emma Bean went too. Most of the time.

But there was the day Molly got her new bike. And the day she went to Peter's house to play. And the time Aunt Rose brought her the doll who could do everything, even hiccup.

Then Emma Bean sat on Molly's bed and waited. She never moved and she never complained. Emma Bean was good at waiting. Besides, she needed a rest.

At night Molly always came back. "*Pssst,*" she whispered into Emma Bean's long soft ears. "*Andthen—andthen...*"

And Molly told Emma Bean everything about her day.

Molly had a bad day. She spilled her milk. She wrote on the wall. She slammed the door. And she wouldn't say she was sorry.

Molly's mother sent her to her room.

"Mommy doesn't love me," she told Emma Bean. "We will run away and never come back."

She packed her pillow and pajamas and crayons and motorcycle.

"Good-bye forever," said Molly. And she closed the door.

The night was big and black. Snowflakes swirled in the wind and landed, icy wet, on their noses.

"Uh-oh," said Molly. "I forgot my boots."

She tiptoed upstairs. And there was her mother waiting for her.

"I'm sorry I scolded you," she said.

"I'm sorry about the milk," said Molly. "And the wall."

The three of them had hot chocolate. Molly's mother helped her unpack. Then she tucked Molly and Emma Bean into bed.

Outside the wind howled and the snow fell. But in Molly's bed Molly and Emma Bean were snuggly warm.

Soon after Molly turned five, it was the first day of school.

She walked along, singing a little song. "School is fun. I'm not scared. School is fun. I am brave." But she held Emma Bean very tight.

At school Molly painted a picture of the sun and wrote her ABC's. That was fun. But she couldn't talk unless she raised her hand and there were big boys who pushed. That was not fun.

And she didn't have a friend.

In the play kitchen Molly made a birthday cake with five candles.

"Can we have a bite?" asked someone.

That was how Molly met Sara Louise. And Emma Bean met a bear named Gloria.

They went outside to the playground. They all had fast rides on the long shiny slide. Then Molly and Sara Louise climbed high in the jungle gym. Emma Bean and Gloria sat under a tree and watched.

On the way home Molly skipped. "School is fun," she sang. "I was brave. School is fun. I have a friend."

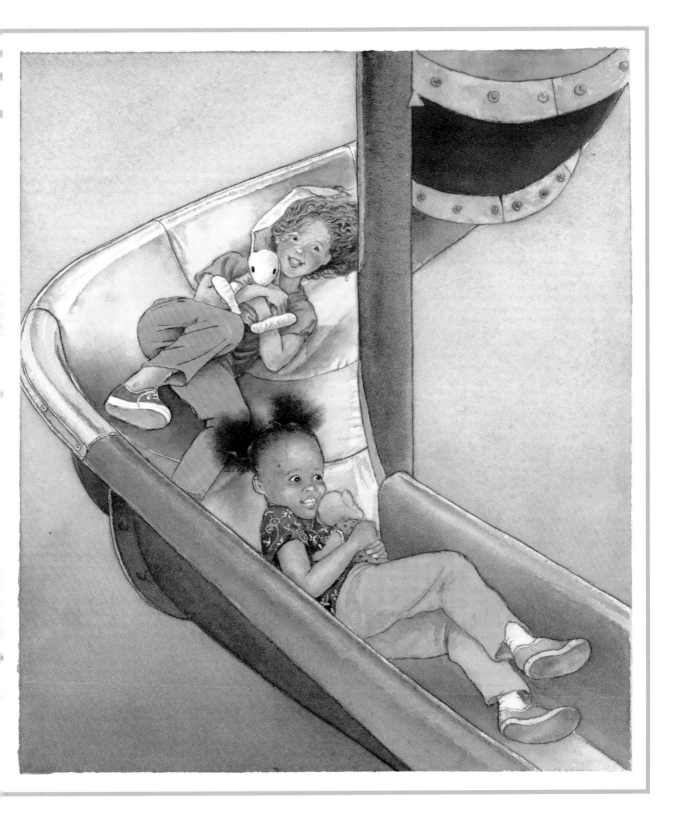

One day Molly's grandmother came to visit.

"Would you sew Emma Bean's elbow?" asked Molly.

Stitch, stitch. Snip, snip. Those hands felt so familiar.

"What has happened to poor Emma Bean?" her grandmother asked. "She looks all worn out."

"Well," said Molly, "her ear is bent from flying. The pink stains are strawberries and the purple ones are grape juice. The stitches are from when she fell out of a tree. I don't know how she lost her whiskers."

"What are we going to do with her?" asked Molly's grandmother.

"Nothing," said Molly. "I like her just the way she is. And I am going to keep her forever."

"Forever?" said her grandmother.

"Forever," said Molly.

Once there was a rabbit and she had a girl.

The girl's name was Molly.

The rabbit was Emma Bean.